The Berenstain Bears®
and the
JUMP ROPE CONTEST

Stan & Jan Berenstain

A GOLDEN BOOK • NEW YORK
Western Publishing Company, Inc., Racine, Wisconsin 53404

Brother Bear was very good
at sports and games.

He was good at football.

He was good at basketball.

2

He was good at soccer.

He was good at baseball.

Sister Bear was good at those things, too. But she was smaller than Brother and younger. So she could not do those things as well as Brother.

There was one thing Sister *could* do better than Brother. That was jump rope. She could jump rope much better than Brother.

She could jump.

She could skip.

She could hop.

She could jump slowly.

She could jump fast.

She could jump
very, very fast.

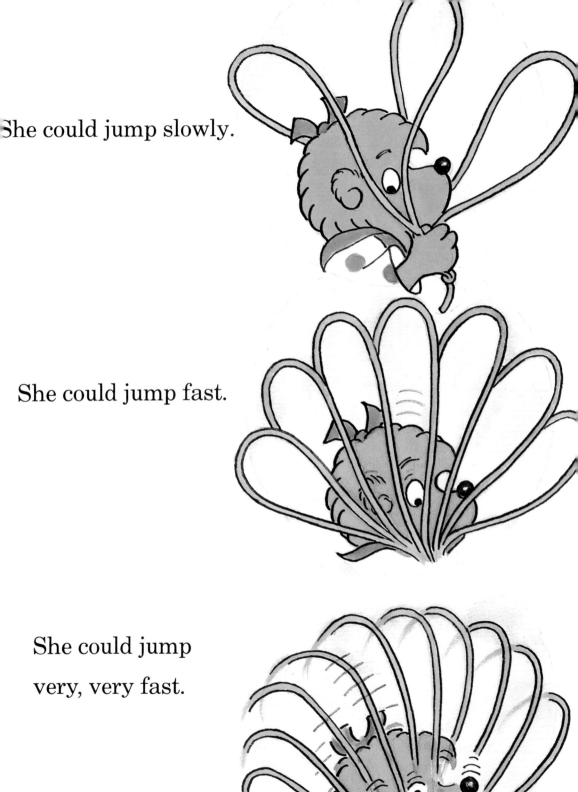

Sister was proud of her rope
jumping. She was so proud of
her rope jumping that she began
to boast a little.

"I am the best rope jumper in Bear
Country!" she said.

She began to boast a lot.

"I am the best rope jumper in the
whole wide world!" she said.

It was quite a boast. But one day
she got a chance to prove her boast.

"Look!" said Papa. "It says in the
newspaper that there is going to be
a big jump rope contest at the
playground!"

Sister said, "I'm going to enter that contest and *prove* that I'm the best rope jumper in the whole wide world!"

"It's not a good idea to be so boastful," said Mama.

"Why not?" asked Sister.

"Because there may be someone who is a better rope jumper than you," said Mama.

"Not a chance," said Sister.
"Watch this!" Then she jumped
rope so fast, she was a blur.

The day of the contest
came. All the jumpers were
there with their jump ropes.
The winner would be the one
who jumped the longest.

"Ready, get set, jump!" said
the judge.

Sister outjumped Lizzy.

She outjumped Queenie.

She outjumped Babs.

18

One by one, all the other jumpers dropped out. It looked as if Sister would be the winner.

But, wait! There was still one other jumper! It was Mr. Frog! Where had *he* come from?

Mr. Frog had hopped out of the woods with his little green jump rope. Now he and Sister were the only ones still jumping. And it was starting to get dark!

Sister and Mr. Frog jumped and
jumped and jumped and jumped. Sister
was getting tired. Her legs began to
hurt. Her arms began to hurt. She was
beginning to hurt all over.

Mr. Frog looked as fresh as a daisy.
He looked as if he could jump all night
and the next day, too!

Sister looked worried. But
Brother had an idea. "Keep
jumping, Sister! Keep jumping!"
he shouted. "It's getting dark!"

Sister didn't understand.
What did getting dark have to
do with anything?

What it had to do with was *lightning bugs*! Lots of lightning bugs were coming out!

Mr. Frog just *loved* lightning bugs! Soon he stopped thinking about jumping and began thinking about lightning bugs. He shot out his long sticky tongue at a yummy lightning bug.

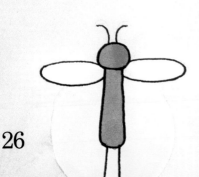

But he missed! His long sticky tongue got tangled in his little green jump rope.

Mr. Frog fell to the ground in a sticky green tangle. Sister kept right on jumping.

"Hurray! Sister wins!" shouted
everyone.

Sister learned a lesson that night: You don't have to be the best in the whole wide world to be a winner. You just have to keep jumping.

WINNER